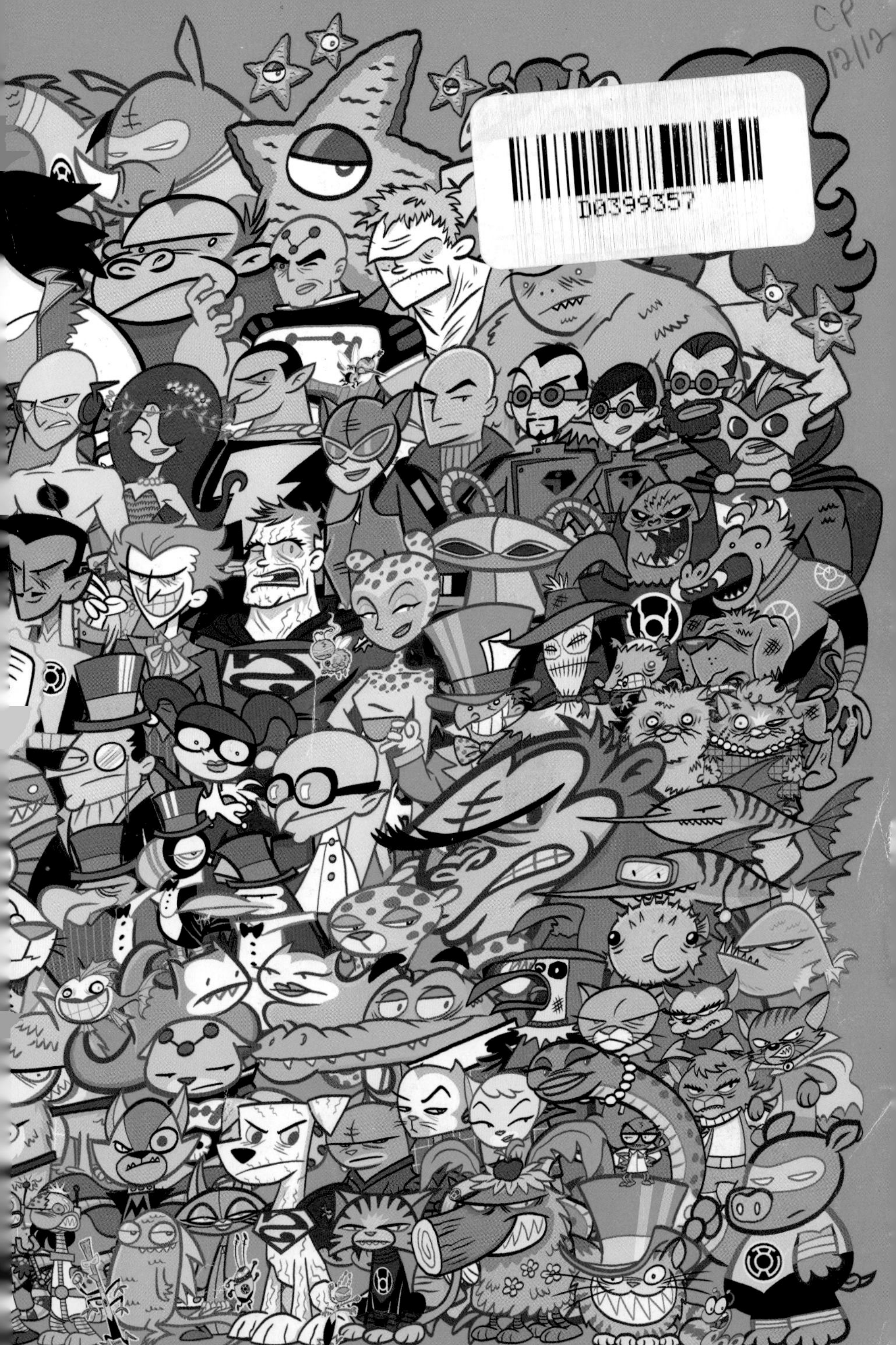

DC™

SUPER-PETS!

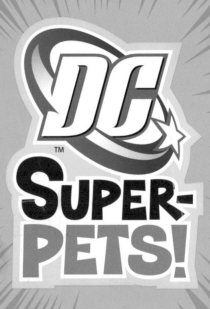

by Sarah Hines
Stephens

NIGHT OF THE SCAREDY CROWS

illustrated by
Art Baltazar

Batman created by Bob Kane

Picture Window Books
a capstone imprint

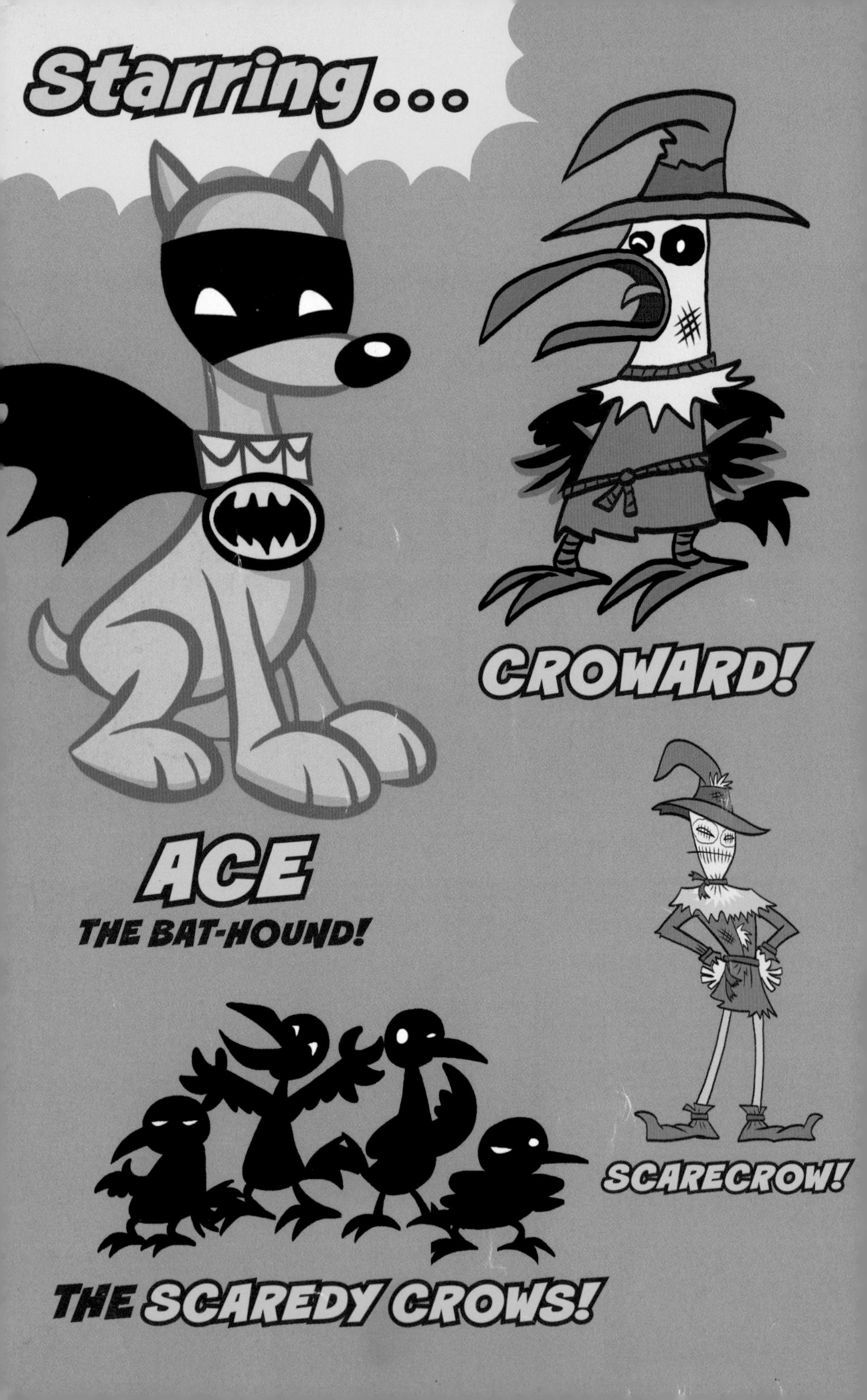
Starring...
ACE
THE BAT-HOUND!
CROWARD!
SCARECROW!
THE SCAREDY CROWS!

TABLE OF CONTENTS!

SUPER-PET HERO FILE 005:
ACE

Ultra-hearing

Ultra-smell

Bat-cowl

Utility Collar

Fireproof Cape

Bat-Symbol

Powerful Paws

Super Hero Owner:
BATMAN

Species: Bat-Hound

Place of Birth: Gotham

Age: Unknown

Favorite Food: Crime Fighter Crunchies

Bio: Batman found Ace while solving a case. The Bat-Hound considers himself Batman's partner, *not* his pet.

Super-Pet Enemy File 020:
CROWARD

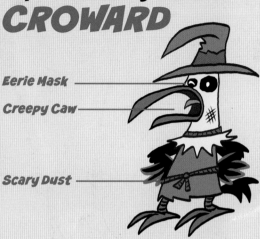

Eerie Mask

Creepy Caw

Scary Dust

Super-Pet Enemy File 020B:
SCAREDY CROWS

Beady Eyes

Shadowy Figures

Super-villain Owner:
SCARECROW

SPOOKY SEASON

Ace the Bat-Hound stepped out of the **Batcave.** He looked up at the harvest moon and breathed in the chilly fall air. The World's Greatest Dog Detective let out a long, happy *HOWL.* Then he set out to patrol Gotham City.

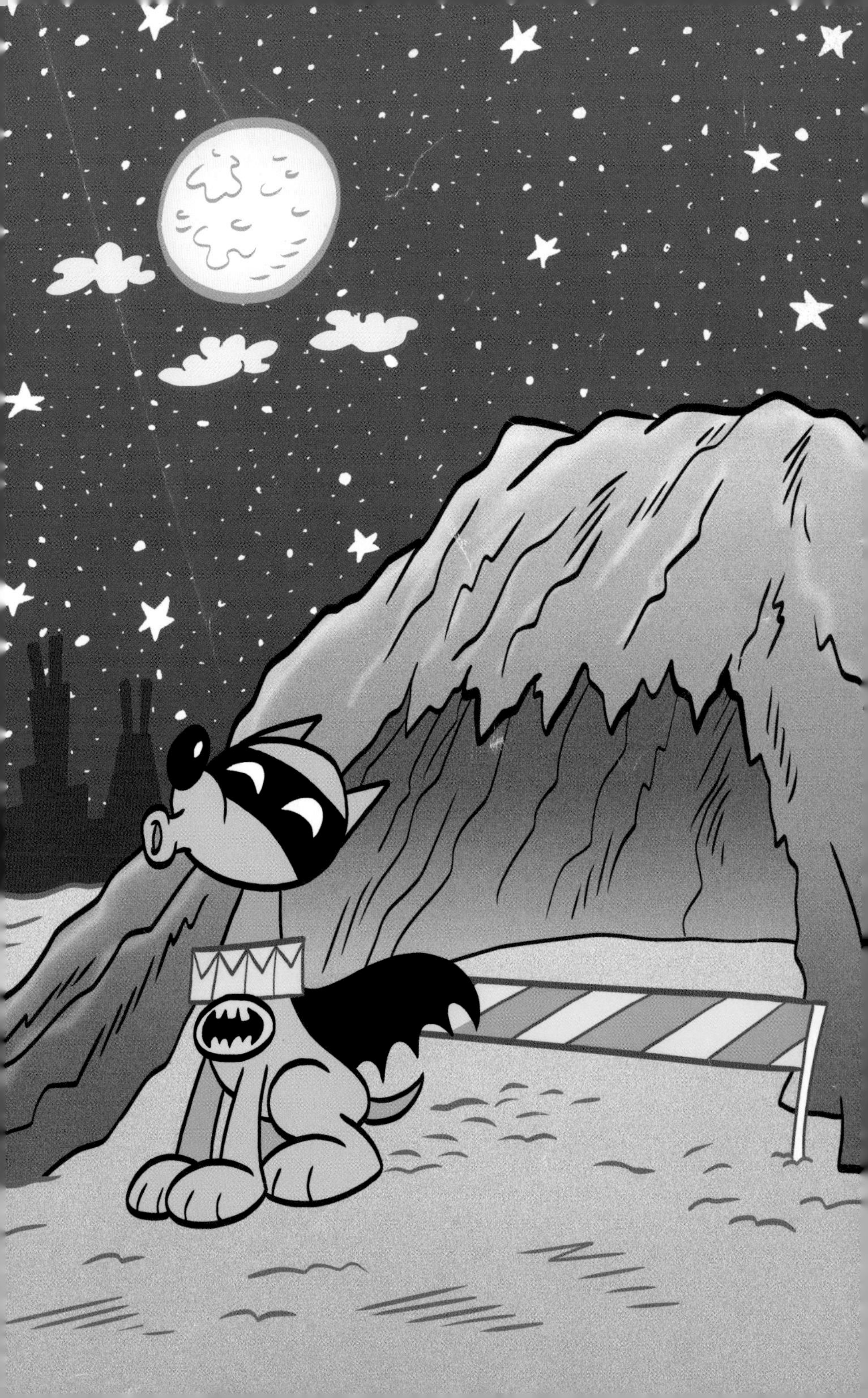

Ace enjoyed crunching through the autumn leaves. **Batman's** loyal Super-Pet loved everything about this time of year. He loved the changing season, the weather, and especially . . .

Halloween!

Halloween was Ace's favorite holiday. What could be better than a day devoted to costumes, celebrating after dark, and getting treats?

Nothing! Ace thought.

The Bat-Hound took another deep breath. He wanted to enjoy the scents of the season, but — wait a second!

The Dog Detective froze in his tracks. He sniffed again and again.

SNIFF! SNIFF! SNIFF!

Ace had a powerful nose. He had keen eyes. He had sensitive ears, too. The Bat-Hound often used his ultra-sharp senses to detect sneaky criminals and catch clever crooks.

But tonight, it was what Ace *couldn't* detect that stopped him cold.

With his ears up, his eyes peeled, and his nose working overtime, Ace raced through the streets. But no matter where he went, the Bat-Hound couldn't smell pumpkin guts or roasting seeds.

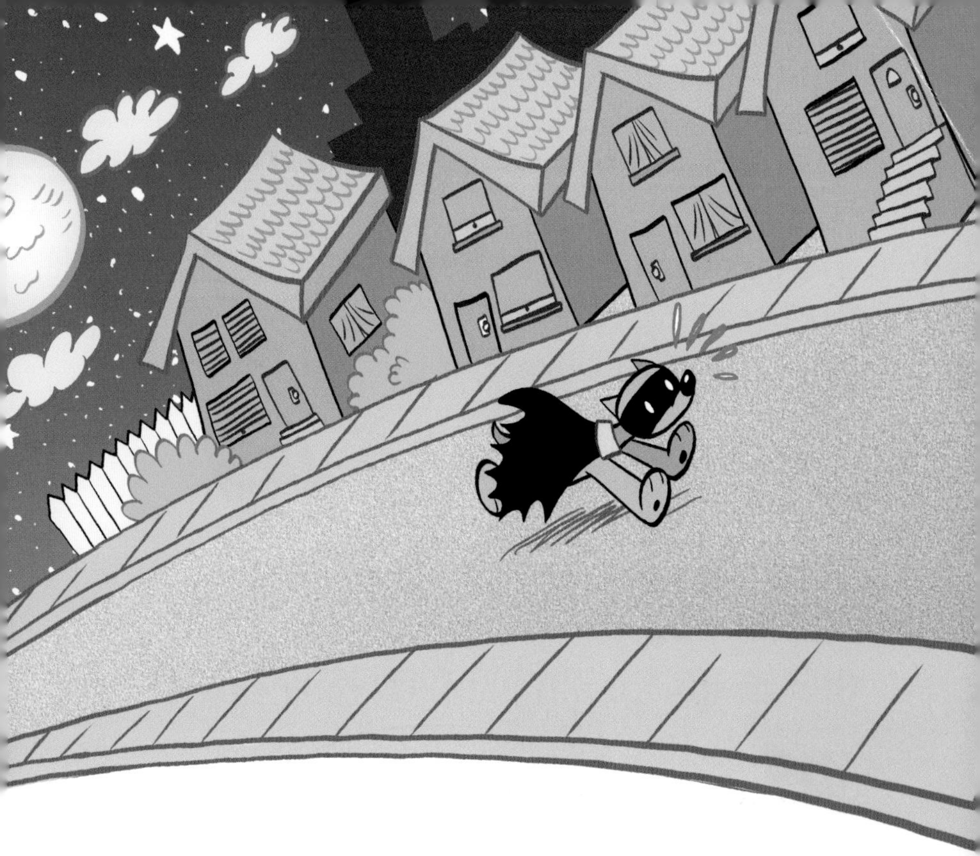

Ace couldn't see skeletons or spider webs decorating doorways. He didn't hear giggling kids readying their costumes. In fact, there weren't even any kids playing outside!

Something's wrong, Ace thought.

Why did every home in Gotham City seem to have their doors shut tight? **Ace needed to get to the bottom of this mystery!** 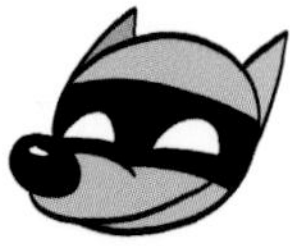

Silently, the Bat-Hound prowled the streets for clues. With only one day until Halloween, the children should have been playing games and ignoring their parents' calls to come home. They should have been partying, bobbing for apples, running in hay mazes, and jumping in leaves.

But nobody was out and about!

All Ace could find were fallen leaves and a few black feathers . . .

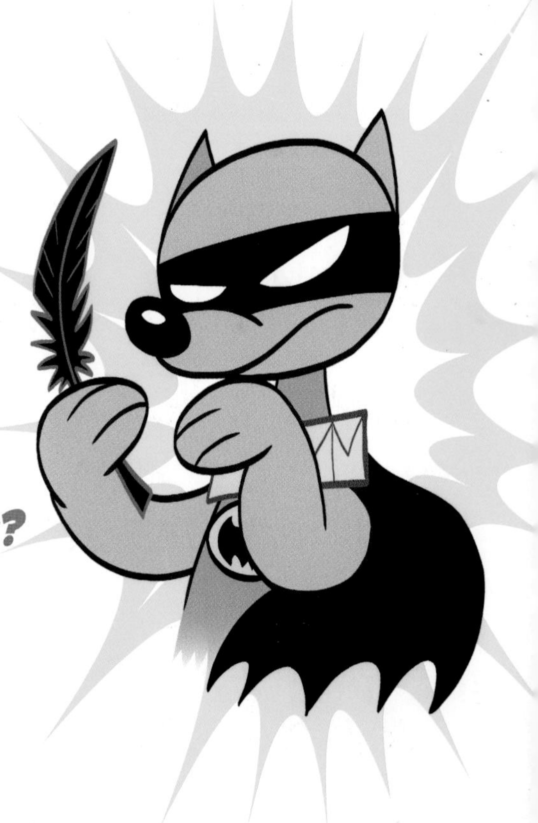

Black feathers? Ace wondered.

The Bat-Hound picked up one of the fallen feathers. ***Perhaps this is a clue,*** he thought.

The dark plumes littered the sidewalks. Ace walked from one to another. The feathers seemed to be leading in one direction.

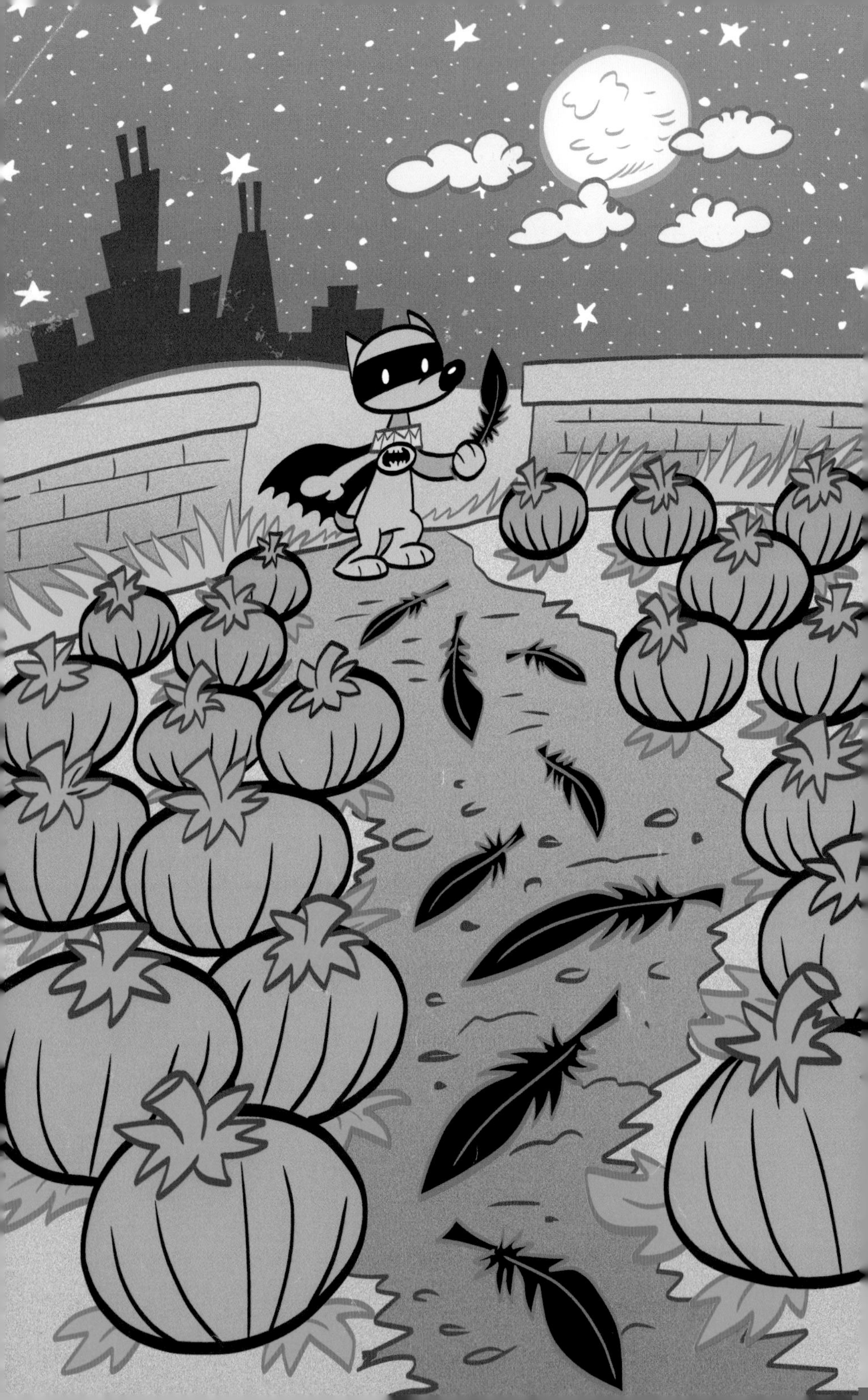

The Bat-Hound followed the trail of feathers to the edge of the city. It took him right to Peter Pumpkin Eater's Pumpkin Patch.

Peter's was the largest patch in the city. Every year, children bought pumpkins from Peter's to carve into jack-o'-lanterns. On the night before Halloween, the patch was usually picked clean. Not this year! Hundreds of pumpkins remained in the fields.

"Has Halloween been canceled?!" shouted Ace.

FEATHERED FIENDS

WHoOOOOOOOOOOOO!

Wind blew leaves from trees and

rustled cornstalks. Although Ace

seemed to be alone, the Bat-Hound

knew he wouldn't be for long. The

feathers had stopped here for a reason.

Whoever dropped these must be nearby, Ace thought. The Bat-Hound ducked behind a giant pumpkin and waited for the suspect.

CAW! CAW! The Bat-Hound was right. Suddenly, a murder of crows lifted off from a nearby cornfield.

The birds screeched and pumped their jet-black wings.

As they took to the skies, Ace noticed something strange. A cloud of green dust fell from their flapping feathers. The dust spread out on the wind. It drifted down to the ground, covering everything in a toxic green layer.

The Bat-Hound sniffed the dust, and chills ran up his spine. **BRRR!** Ace shuddered and suddenly felt . . . afraid!

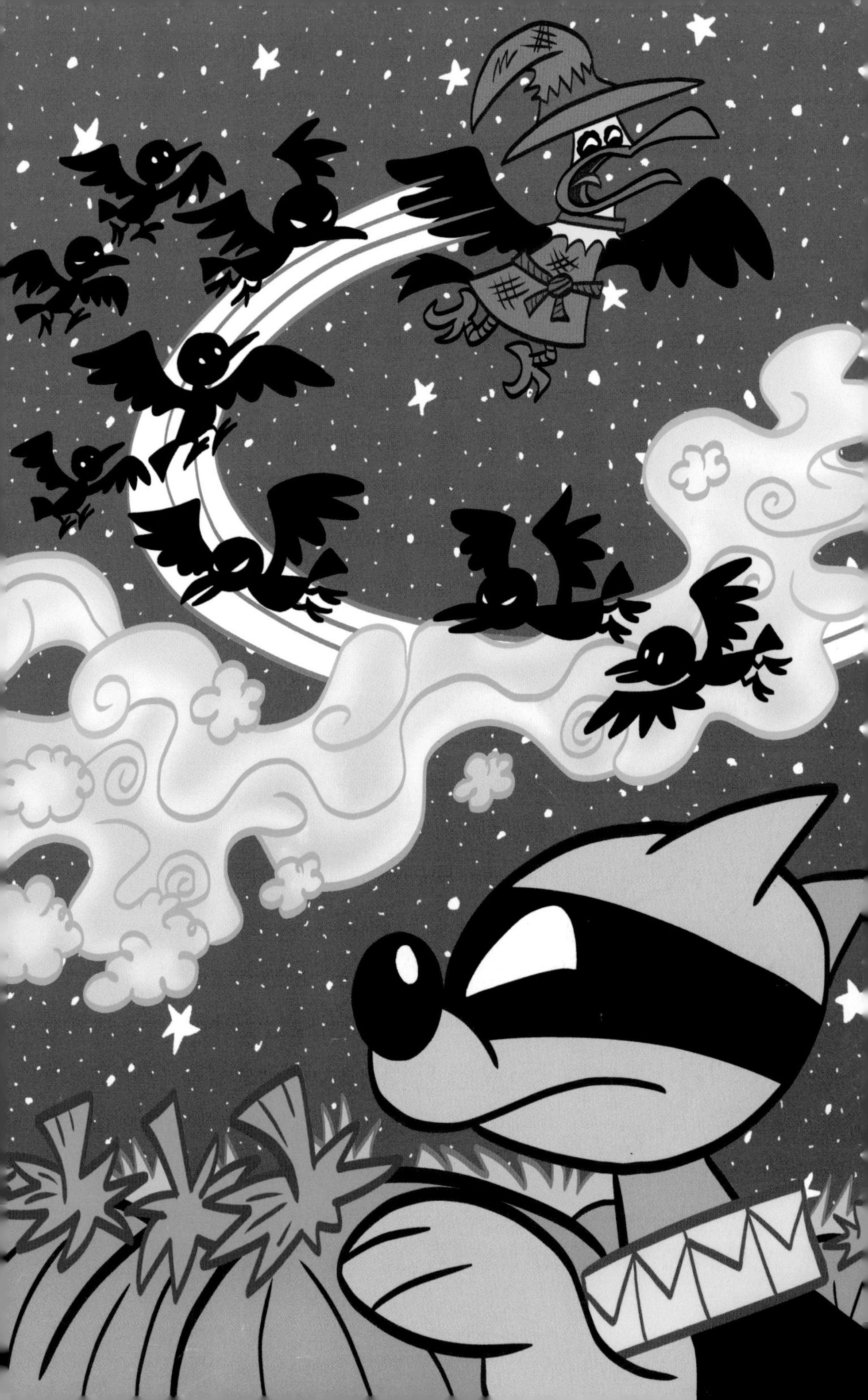

Fear was not something Ace was used to, but he felt it now. He had the chills. His teeth chattered. All around him shadows began to look like his worst nightmares!

Ace didn't like the creepy feeling. He wanted to run and hide under a bed. But Ace was no scaredy dog!

FWIP! FWIP! FWIP!

The Bat-Hound tried shaking off the fear.   **"Those birds must have done this to me!"** he exclaimed.

Ace studied the creepy crows. The black birds were ragged and spooky. They were no ordinary birds. They could only belong to one man . . .

"The **Scarecrow!**" Ace growled.

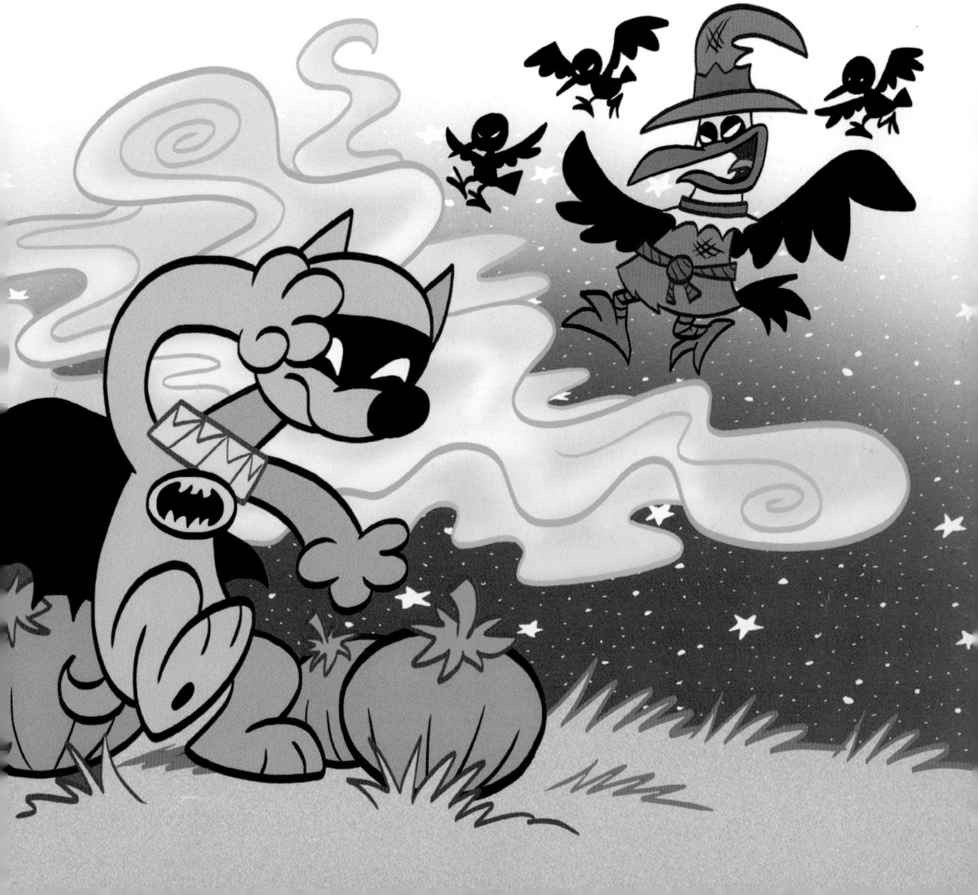

The Bat-Hound tried not to whine when he thought of Batman's enemy. The Scarecrow was a brilliant doctor gone bad. His evil potions made people's greatest fears come to life.

The bad birds flying toward the center of the city were doing the same thing! The dust that flew off their feathers and spread over the town was making Ace shiver.

And it was making everyone else afraid of Halloween!

BEEP!

Ace pushed a button on his collar, turning on a gas mask. He didn't want to breathe any more scaredy powder.

With the mask on, Ace took a deep breath. Instantly, his chills were gone. His teeth stopped chattering.

The Bat-Hound was ready to get his jaws on one of those evil birds. But they were already flying away.

Ace watched the flock get smaller in the sky. He wished he could soar after them like **Krypto the Super-Dog,** but Ace couldn't fly. Luckily, he had more than a few tricks up his collar.

BEEEEP! Ace launched a **Batarang** attached to a **Batrope.**

The Batarang flew from Ace's collar and wrapped around a nearby lamppost. Ace was airborne! Using the rope, he swung himself into the middle of the flock. The crows scattered in every direction.

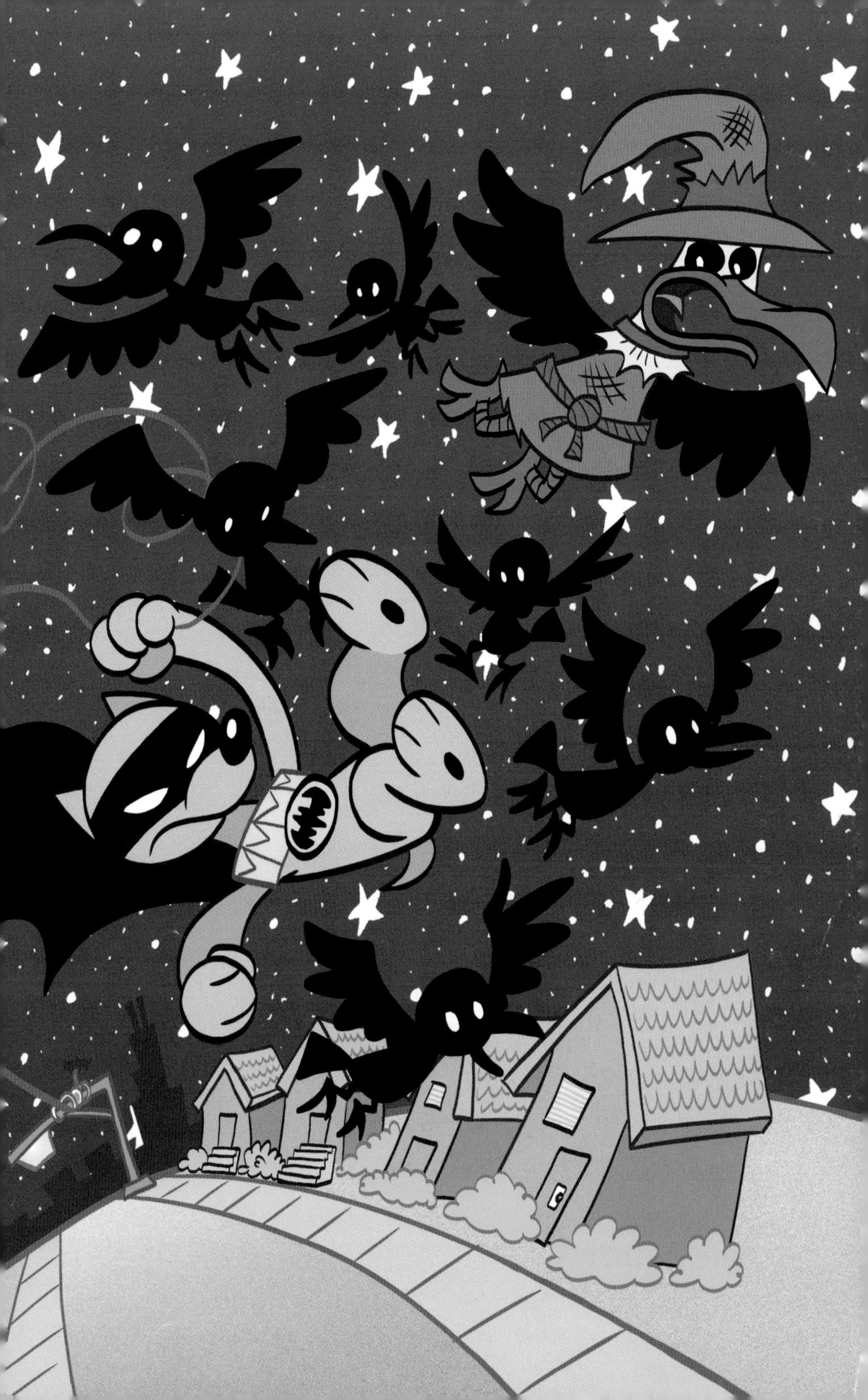

Ace clamped his teeth around the biggest bird and hung on tight. The two of them tumbled out of the sky.

WHAM! They landed on the street. The crow was surprised to find himself nose to beak with the Bat-Hound.

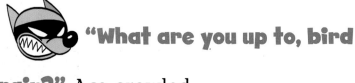 **"What are you up to, bird brain?"** Ace growled.

The big crow stared back at him with beady eyes. His name was **Croward**. The feathered fiend was the leader of the flock. "You can't make me squawk, dog," he screeched.

Ace kept a paw on Croward and an eye on the sky. The rest of Croward's flock was flying back to see what had happened to their leader. They flew in circles around Ace, cawing and flapping their wings.

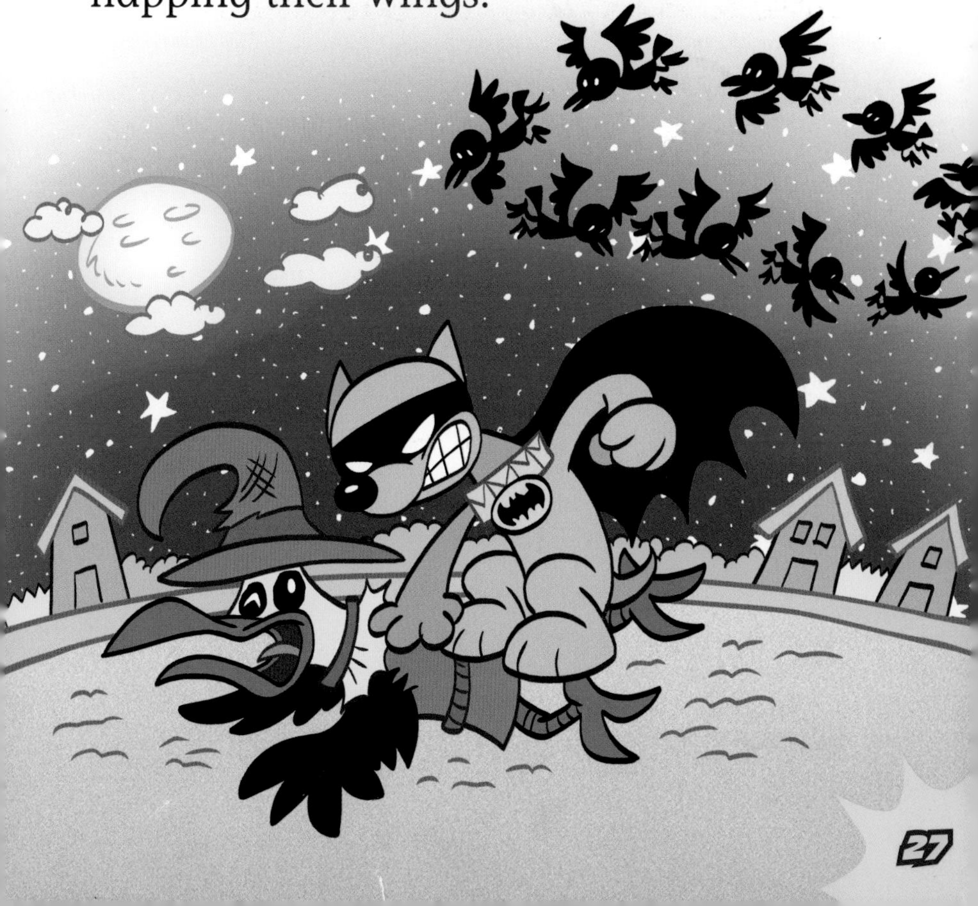

The Scaredy Crows quickly created

a toxic green cloud to scare Ace off.

But their frightful dust was useless on

him now. It didn't have any effect on

Croward either.

"Trick for treats! Trick for treats!" the

crows cawed as they circled closer.

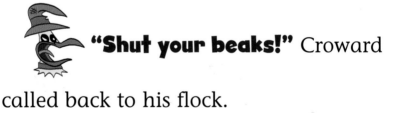 **"Shut your beaks!"** Croward

called back to his flock.

But it was too late. The crows had

given Ace a clue. The Bat-Hound

quickly realized what they were after.

The Scaredy Crows were trying to "trick" kids into staying inside on Halloween. Then they planned to steal all of the treats for themselves!

 **RUFF! RUFF!** "I'm on to you, Scaredy Crows!" Ace barked.

Unfortunately, the crows were also onto him.

In a great flap of feathers, they swarmed Ace, grabbing his ears and tail. They lifted him off of Croward and up into the air.

Higher and higher the crows climbed, pulling Ace along with them. The Bat-Hound watched the city grow smaller and smaller below him. He wasn't afraid of heights, but the wild ride was making the dog dizzy.

Ace had no chance of escape. Even if he could reach his collar, the Super-Pet wouldn't have anywhere to attach a Batrope. He had to think fast.

When the city looked like a toy town far below them, the bird leader snapped his beak. **CRACK!**

Croward's flock obeyed the order. They released Ace all at once. Ace fell toward the ground!

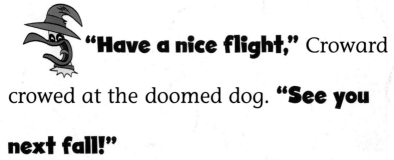 **"Have a nice flight,"** Croward crowed at the doomed dog. **"See you next fall!"**

WHOOSH! Ace fell faster and faster. Wind whistled past his ears. The city grew larger and larger every second.

Ace pressed another button on his Utility Collar. **FWISH!** Two bat-like wings unfolded on either side of him. **FWOOOM!** Instead of heading straight toward the street, Ace tilted his body. He leveled off and soared forward. Perhaps he couldn't fly like other Super-Pets. But thanks to his amazing collar of gadgets, the hero could glide like no other dog.

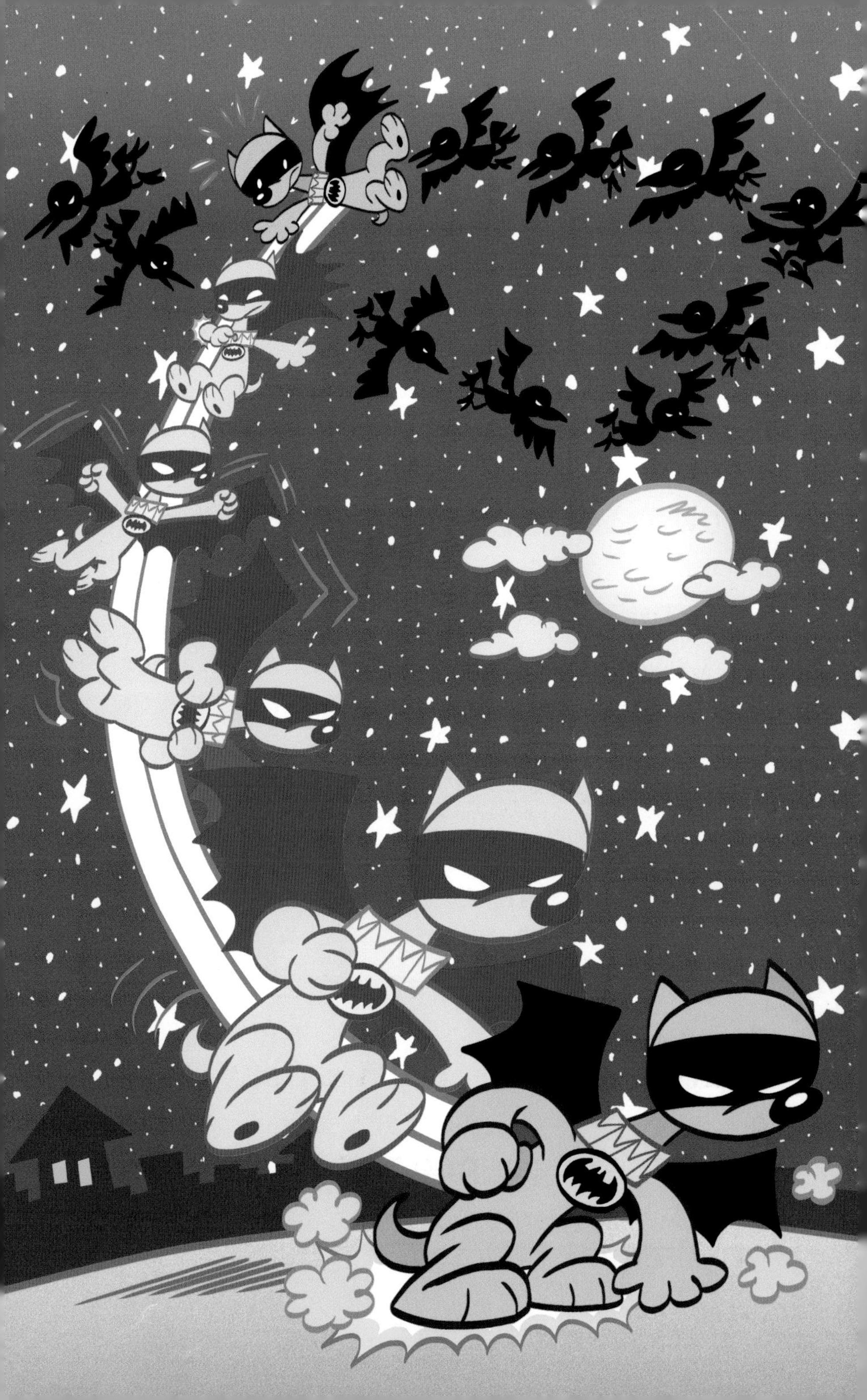

Ace touched down, put away his wings, and quickly hid.

Croward and his cronies soon landed in a nearby cornfield. The crows had no idea they were being watched. They thought Ace was already a goner. But they hadn't seen the last of the masked detective!

Ace ducked behind some cornstalks. He watched the murder of crows puff up their feathers and congratulate themselves. Then suddenly, the evil Scarecrow appeared.

"Is everything going according to plan?" asked the fearsome leader.

"Yes, master," Croward squawked. "The city is scared — too scared to even come outside!"

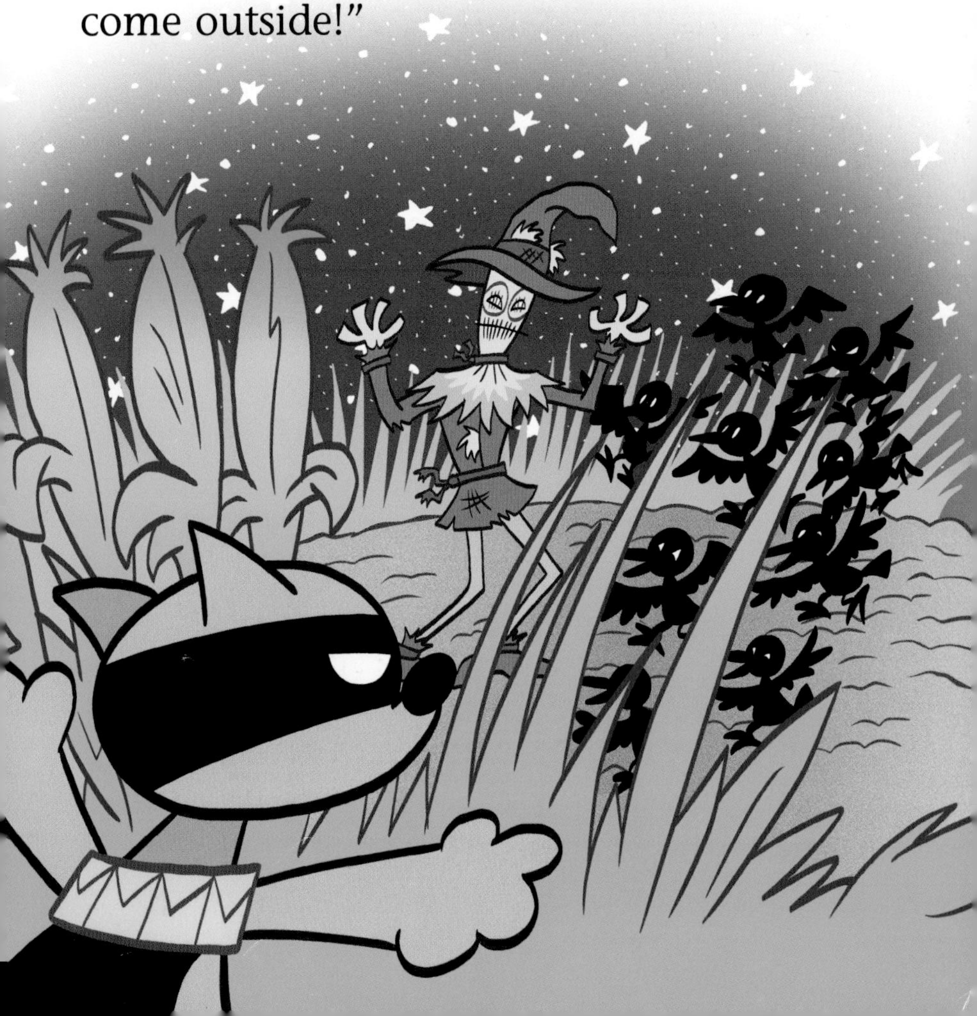

"Excellent," said Scarecrow, grinning madly. "Tomorrow, when it's time to trick-or-treat, the candy will be ours!"

CLACK! CLACK! The other crows snapped their beaks, happily.

"And with all of the glittery foil wrappers, we can make a new Boo Bazooka," added the super-villain. "With two fear cannons, **we can keep the people of Gotham cowering in their houses forever!"**

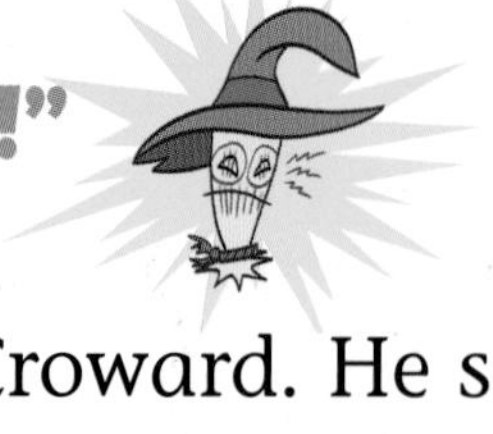

Ace looked behind Croward. He saw something he hadn't noticed before.

It was a cannon made of bits of glittery foil the crows had collected. Beside it were green cannonballs made of the same powder that was on the crows' wings. The crows were planning to blast the city and have the streets — and all of the candy — to themselves!

Ace was going to have to put a stop to their terror.

Tip-toeing out of the field, **the Bat-Hound came up with a plan.**

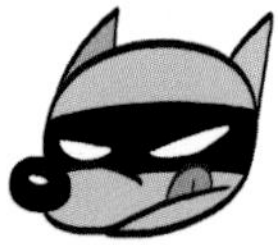

Ace smiled to himself. All he needed to do was trick the crows. Then he'd be able to give the children of Gotham City a real Halloween treat.

TRICKS AND TREATS

The next day, Ace gathered what he needed. He knocked on doors, rang doorbells, and scratched at windows. The frightened people of Gotham were surprised — and a bit scared — to see a masked dog on their doorstep.

"Aren't you early for Halloween?" the people asked. But they knew Ace was a good guy. They helped him get what he needed.

As the sun began to set, Ace dragged a giant sack out to the crows' cornfield. The crows were still asleep with their heads under their wings. They were resting up for a big night.

Beside them, their Boo Bazooka was loaded and aimed at the city. But not for long. Ace turned the cannon . . . and fired right at the crows.

BOOM!

The green ball exploded into a dense cloud that covered the birds. It was so thick they coughed and hacked, choking on the evil potion.

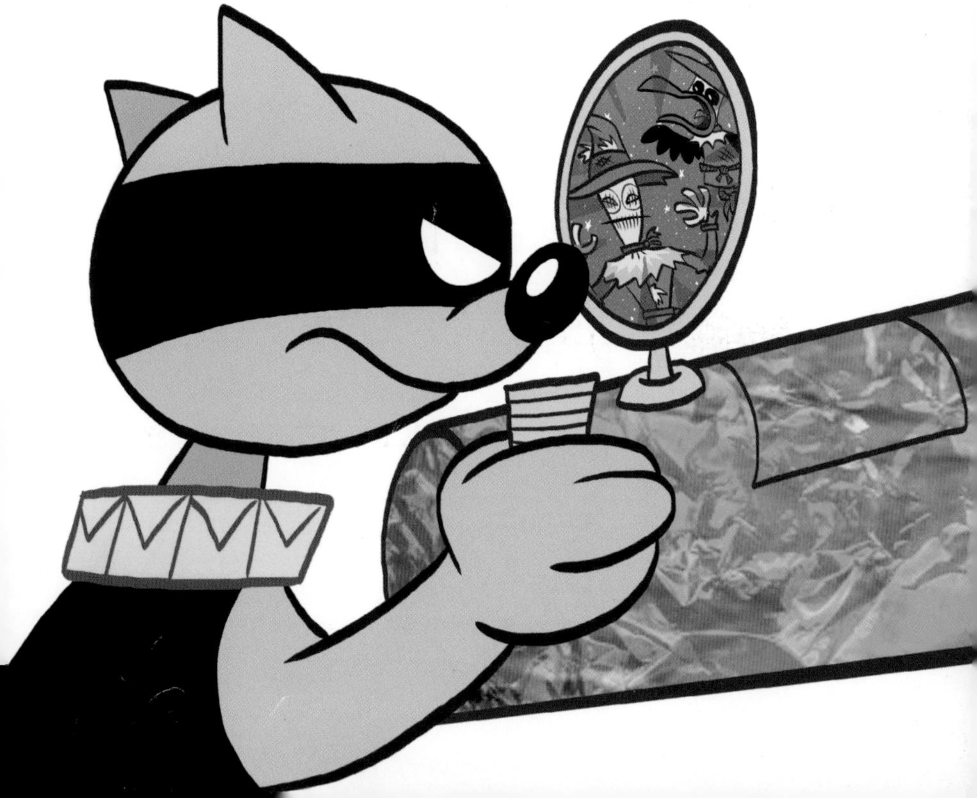

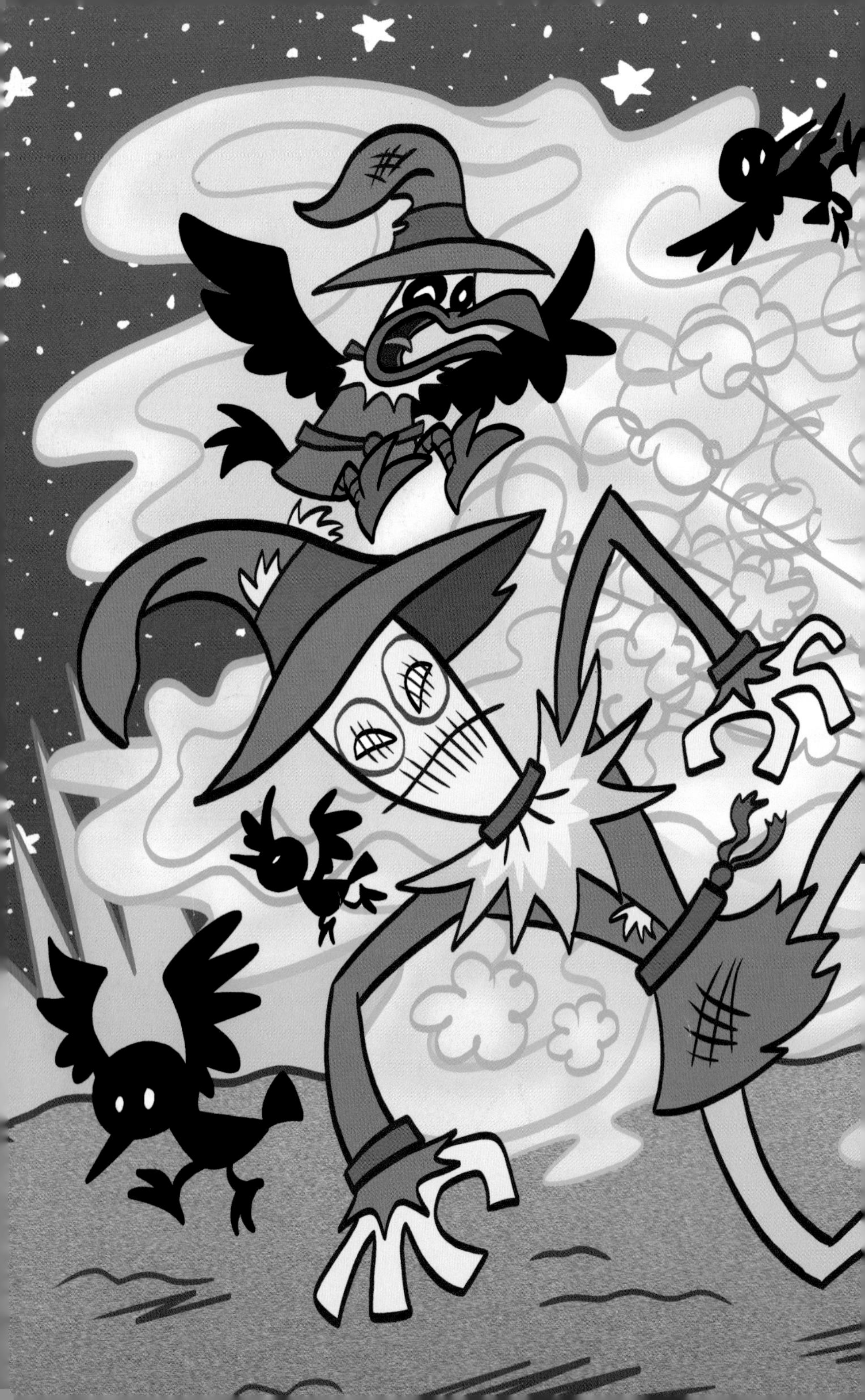

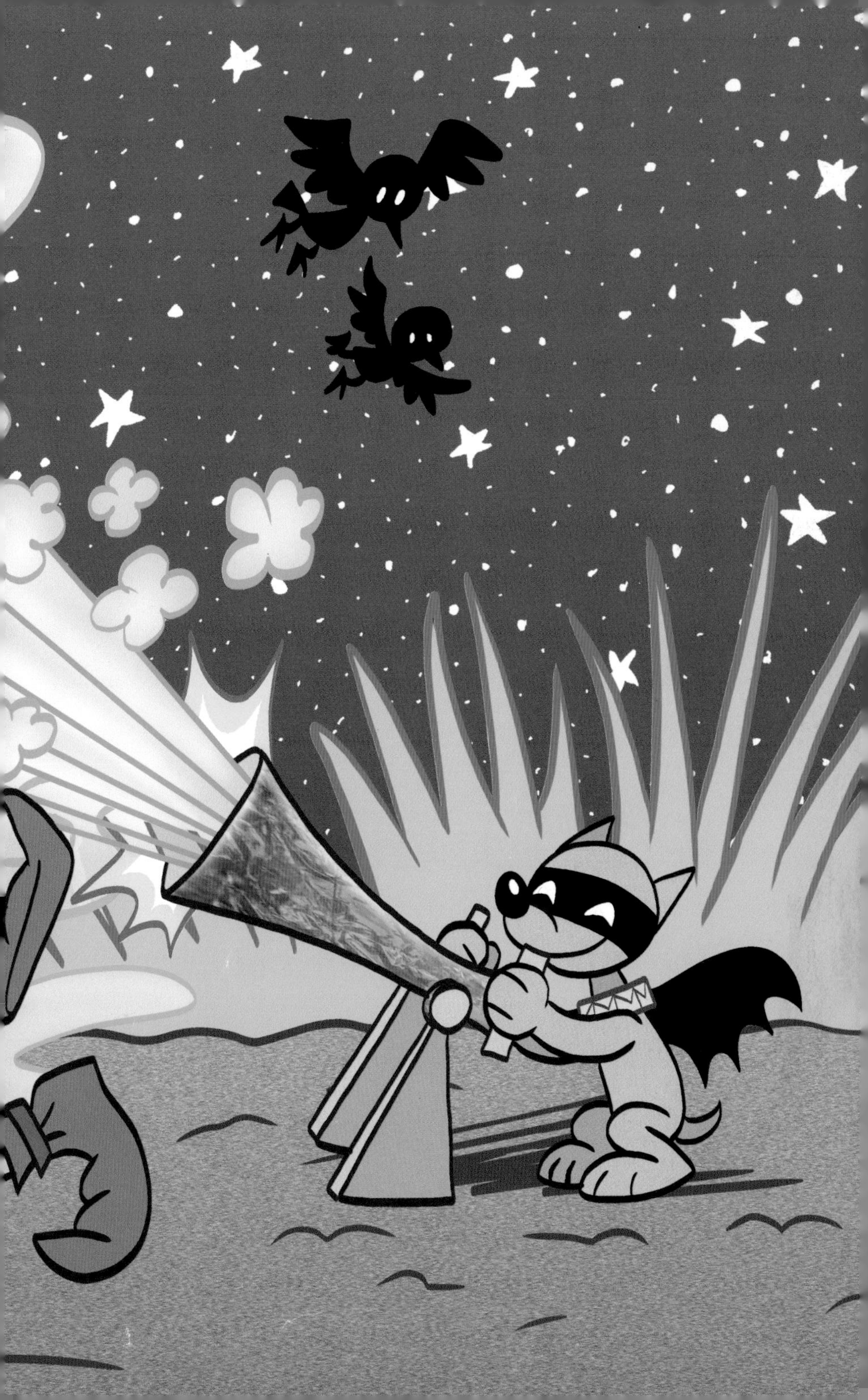

"How do you like the taste of your own medicine?" Ace asked.

The fear dust worked on the crows the same way it had on the people of Gotham. The Scaredy Crows shuddered and screeched, terrified of each other and even their own shadows.

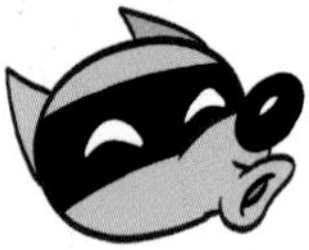

"BOO!" Ace shouted.

The Scaredy Crows were startled. They took to the skies, flying far away from the field and the city. Even the evil Scarecrow fled in fear!

 **"Some crows!"** Ace said, laughing. **"More like a bunch of chickens!"**

Then Ace loaded the bazooka again. Only this time he loaded it with an antidote to fear — candy! He aimed at the city and fired.

KA-BOOOOM!

Thousands of chocolates and colorful candies flew into the air. The treats rained down over the city, falling into chimneys and flying in windows.

Children gobbled the goodies first. When they saw how it made them feel, they gave some to their parents and neighbors and friends. Within moments, the candy cure began to take effect. People's fears disappeared. They felt brave and bold again. They felt happy and carefree!

All over the city, kids scrambled to get into their costumes. They put on face paint and pulled on sheets. Then they stepped outside finally to celebrate Halloween!

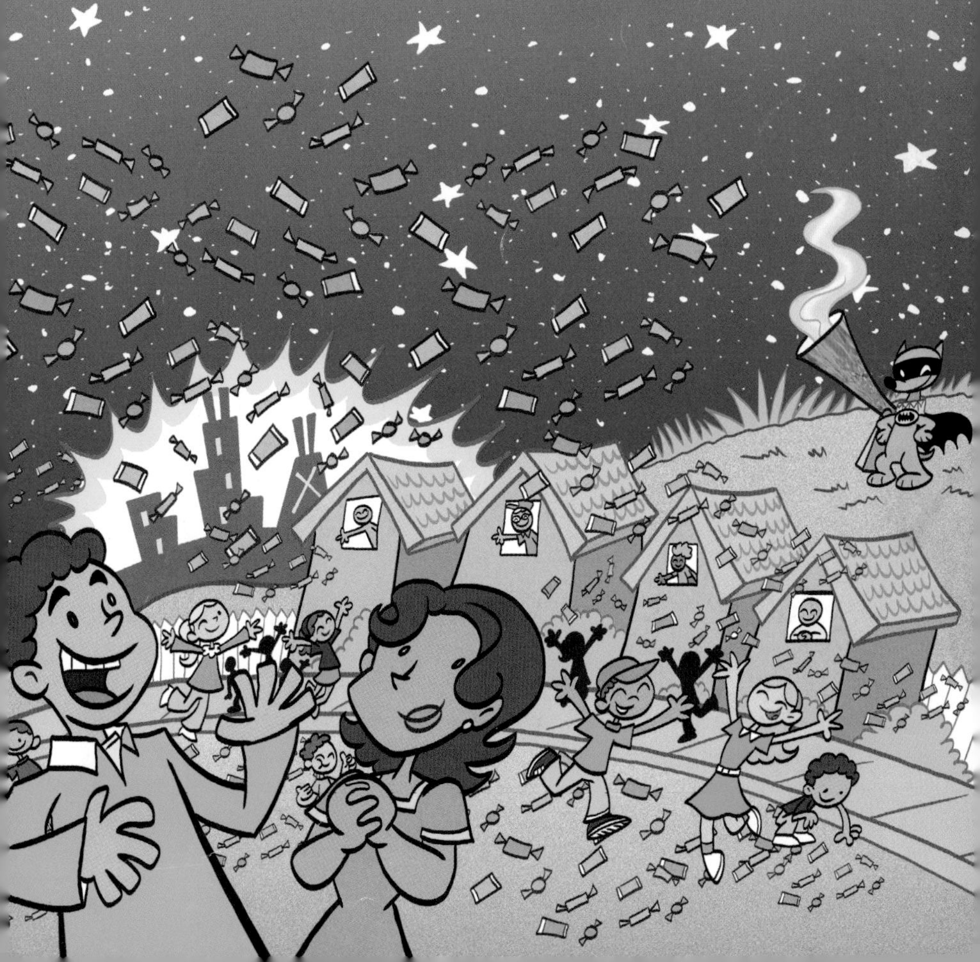

Ace was dog-tired. He headed back to the Batcave, hoping to spend a quiet evening with his owner. But when Ace arrived, the headquarters was dark. The Bat-Hound slowly stepped inside and flicked on the lights.

"Surprise!" came a shout. All around Ace stood his closest friends, ready to celebrate the holiday.

"Did we scare you?" Batman asked his wide-eyed Dog Detective.

"Ha!" laughed Ace the Bat-Hound. "Fear is for the birds!"

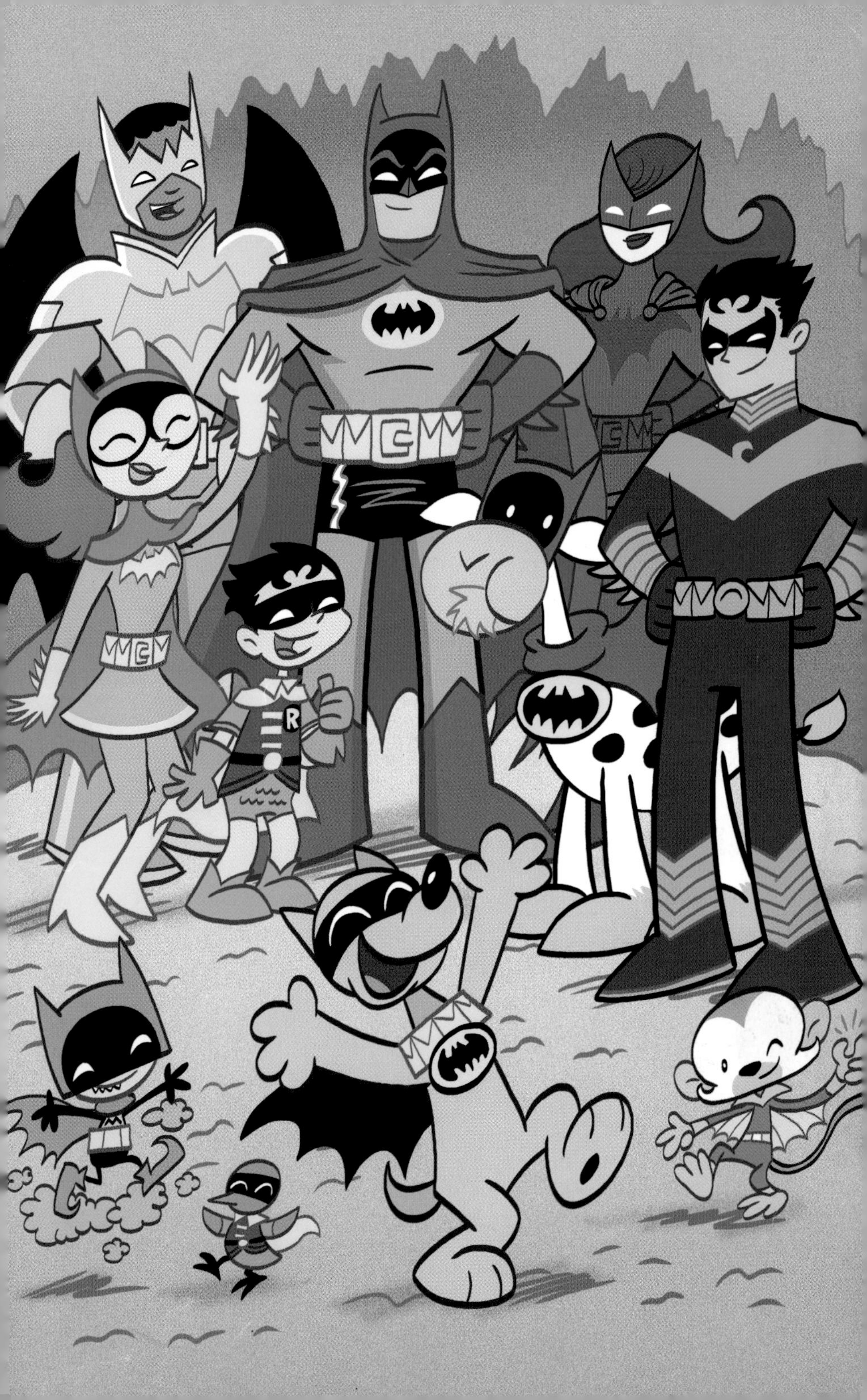

KNOW YOUR HERO PETS!

1. Krypto
2. Streaky
3. Whizzy
4. Comet
5. Beppo
6. Super-Turtle
7. Fuzzy
8. Ace
9. Robin Robin
10. Batcow
11. Jumpa
12. Whatzit
13. Hoppy
14. Tawky Tawny
15. Spot
16. Plastic Frog
17. Gleek
18. Big Ted
19. Dawg
20. Space Dolphins
21. Proty
22. Chameleon Collie
23. Bull Dog
24. Paw Pooch
25. Tusky Husky
26. Hot Dog
27. Tail Terrier
28. Mammoth Mutt
29. Prophetic Pup
30. Rex the Wonder Dog
31. Detective Chimp
32. Starlene
33. Mossy
34. Merle
35. Loafers
36. Storm
37. Topo
38. Ark
39. Fluffy
40. Betty
41. Geoffrey
42. B'dg
43. Sen-Tag
44. Fendor
45. Stripezoid
46. Zallion
47. Ribitz
48. Bzzd
49. Gratch
50. Buzzoo
51. Fossfur
52. Zhoomp
53. Eeny

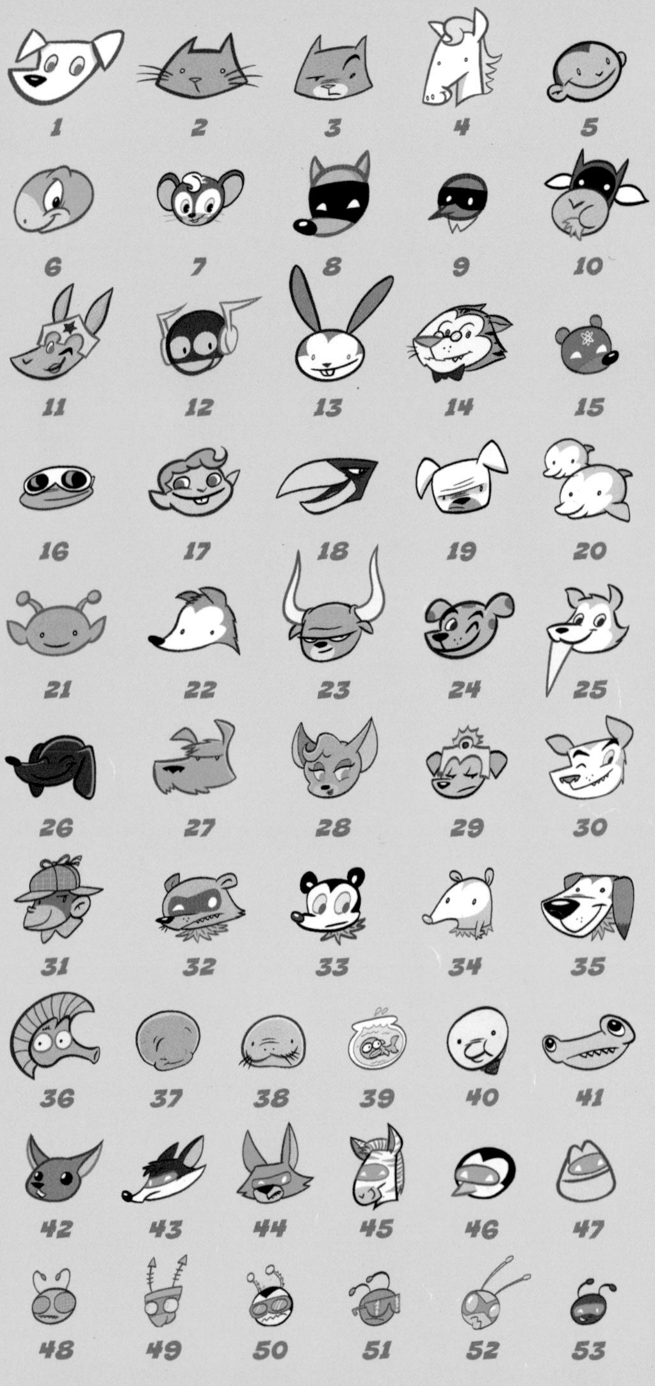
1 2 3 4 5
6 7 8 9 10
11 12 13 14 15
16 17 18 19 20
21 22 23 24 25
26 27 28 29 30
31 32 33 34 35
36 37 38 39 40 41
42 43 44 45 46 47
48 49 50 51 52 53

KNOW YOUR VILLAIN PETS!

1. Bizarro Krypto
2. Ignatius
3. Brainicat
4. Mechanikat
5. Dogwood
6. General Manx
7. Nizz
8. Fer-El
9. Crackers
10. Giggles
11. Artie Puffin
12. Griff
13. Waddles
14. Rozz
15. Mad Catter
16. Croward
17. Chauncey
18. Bit-Bit & X-43
19. Dr. Spider
20. Anna Conda
21. Mr. Mind
22. Sobek
23. Patches
24. Dex-Starr
25. Glomulus
26. Titano
27. Purring Pete
28. Kid Kitty
29. Scratchy Tom
30. Gat-Cat
31. Starro
32. Mama Ripples
33. Faye Precious
34. Limpy
35. Offie Lee
36. Misty
37. Sneezers
38. Johnny
39. Joey
40. Frankie
41. George
42. Whoosh
43. Pronto
44. Snorrt
45. Rolf
46. Squealer
47. Kajunn
48. Tootz
49. Eezix
50. Donald
51. Waxxee
52. Fimble
53. Webbik

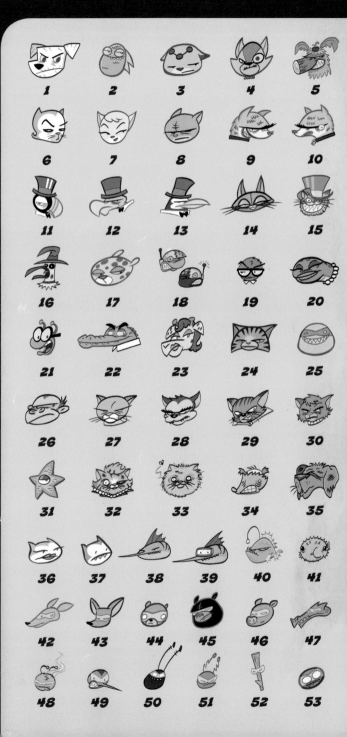

MEET THE AUTHOR!

Sarah Hines Stephens

Sarah Hines Stephens has authored more than 60 books for children and written about all kinds of characters, from Jedi to princesses. When she is not writing, gardening, or saving the world by teaching about recycling, Sarah enjoys spending time with her heroic husband, two kids, and amazing friends.

MEET THE ILLUSTRATOR!

Eisner Award-winner Art Baltazar

Art Baltazar is a cartoonist machine from the heart of Chicago! He defines cartoons and comics not only as an art style, but as a way of life. Currently, Art is the creative force behind *The New York Times* best-selling, Eisner Award-winning, DC Comics series Tiny Titans, and the co-writer for *Billy Batson and the Magic of SHAZAM!* Art is living the dream! He draws comics and never has to leave the house. He lives with his lovely wife, Rose, big boy Sonny, little boy Gordon, and little girl Audrey. Right on!

WORD POWER!

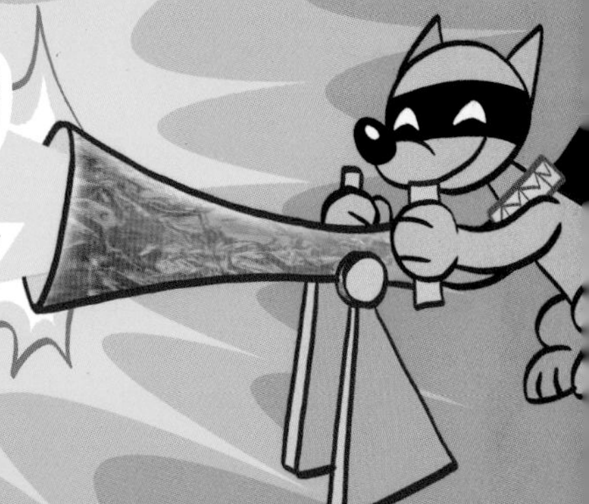

antidote (AN-ti-dote)—something that stops a poison from working

autumn (AW-tuhm)—the season between summer and winter, also known as fall

Batarang (BAT-uh-rayng)—a high-tech weapon used by the Bat-Hound

murder (MUR-dur)—another word for a flock, or group, of crows

patrol (puh-TROHL)—to walk or travel around an area to protect it or to keep watch on people

prowl (PROUL)—to move around quietly and secretly

toxic (TOK-sik)—poisonous, or dangerous to digest

Utility Collar (yoo-TIL-uh-tee KOL-ur)—a thin band worn around the Bat-Hound's neck, which contains all of his secret gadgets

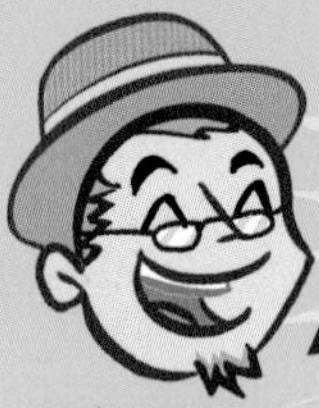

AW YEAH!

ART BALTAZAR SAYS:

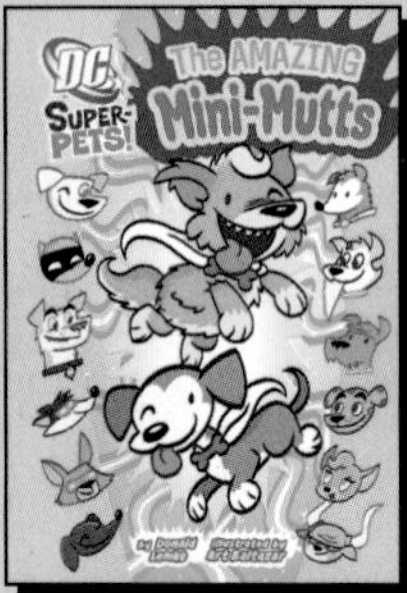
DC SUPER-PETS!
The AMAZING Mini-Mutts

HERO DOGS GALORE!

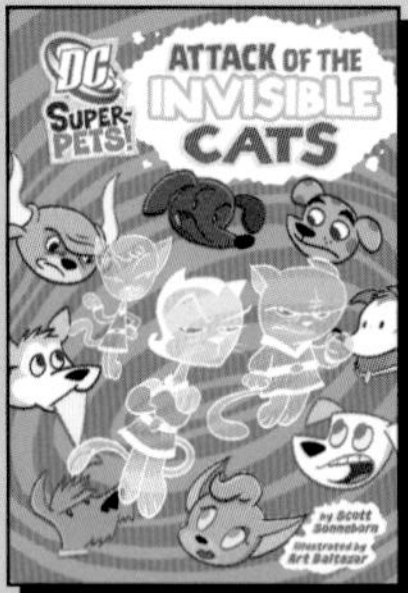
DC SUPER-PETS!
ATTACK OF THE INVISIBLE CATS

SPACE CANINE PATROL AGENCY!

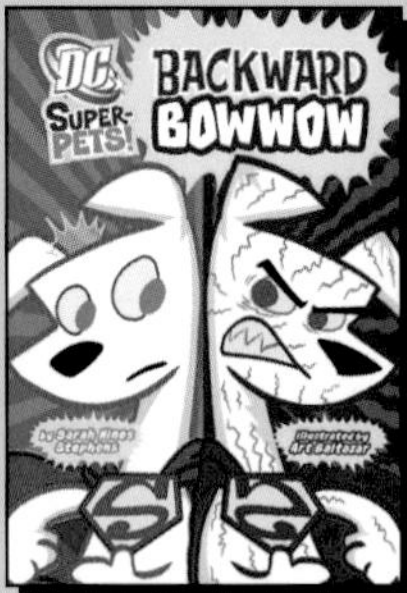
DC SUPER-PETS!
BACKWARD BOWWOW

KRYPTO THE SUPER-DOG!

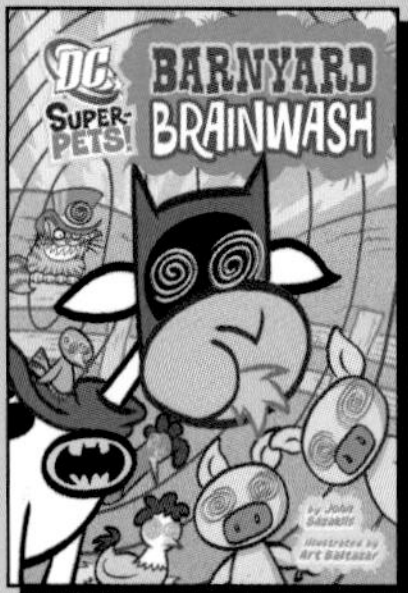
DC SUPER-PETS!
BARNYARD BRAINWASH

BATCOW!

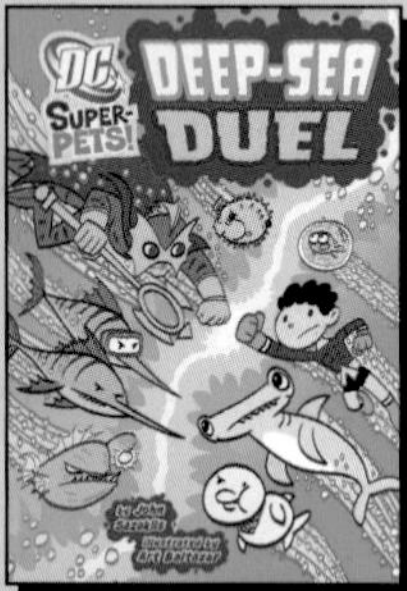
DC SUPER-PETS!
DEEP-SEA DUEL

FLUFFY AND THE AQUA-PETS!

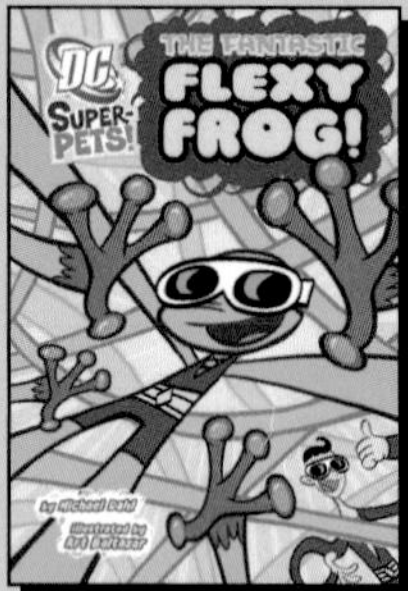
DC SUPER-PETS!
THE FANTASTIC FLEXY FROG!

PLASTIC FROG!

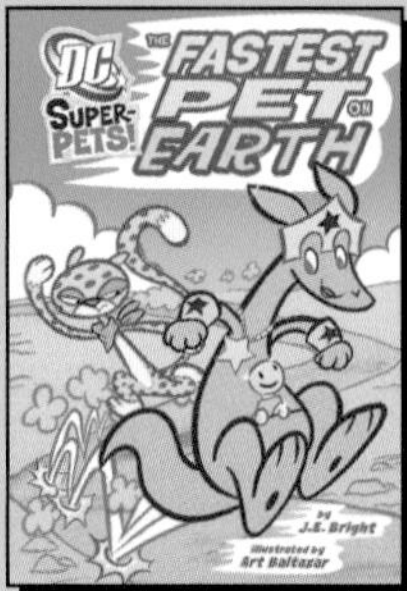
DC SUPER-PETS!
THE FASTEST PET ON EARTH

JUMPA THE KANGA!

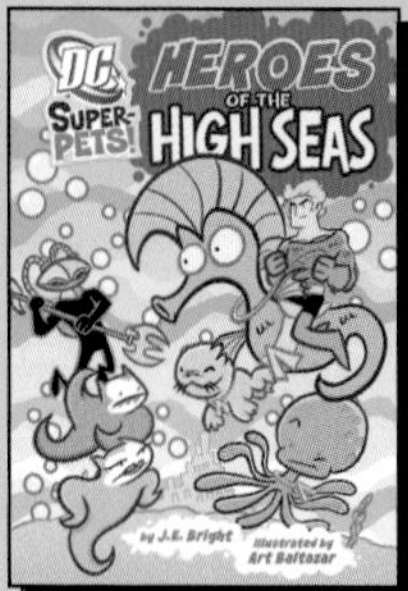
DC SUPER-PETS!
HEROES OF THE HIGH SEAS

STORM AND THE AQUA-PETS!

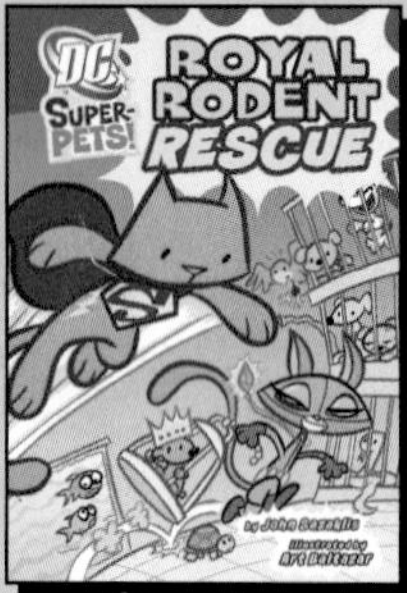
DC SUPER-PETS!
ROYAL RODENT RESCUE

STREAKY THE SUPER-CAT!

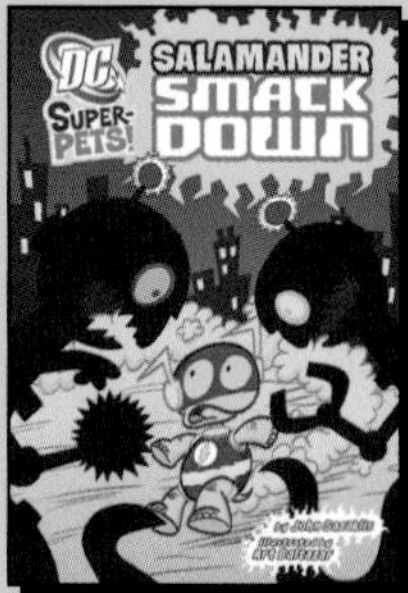
DC SUPER-PETS!
SALAMANDER SMACK DOWN

THE TERRIFIC WHATZIT!

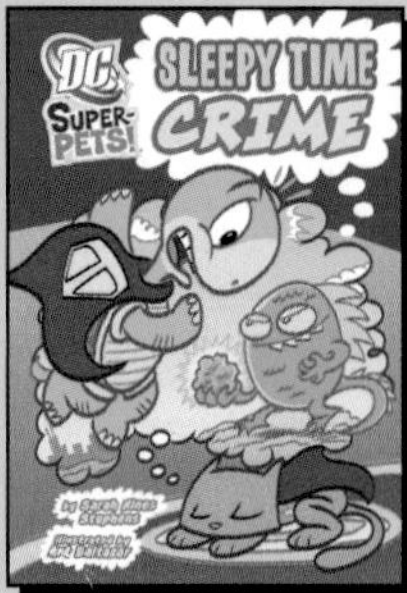
DC SUPER-PETS!
SLEEPY TIME CRIME

SUPER-TURTLE!

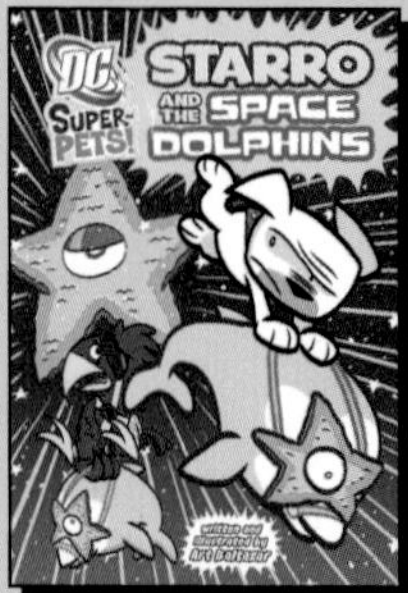
DC SUPER-PETS!
STARRO AND THE SPACE DOLPHINS

BIG TED AND DAWG!

Read all of these totally awesome stories today, starring all of your favorite DC SUPER-PETS!

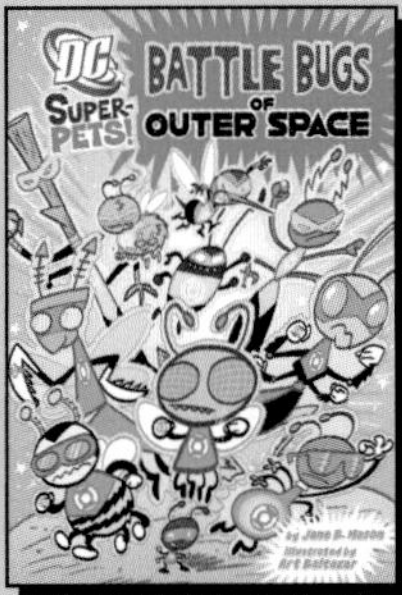
DC SUPER-PETS!
BATTLE BUGS OF OUTER SPACE

GREEN LANTERN BUG CORPS!

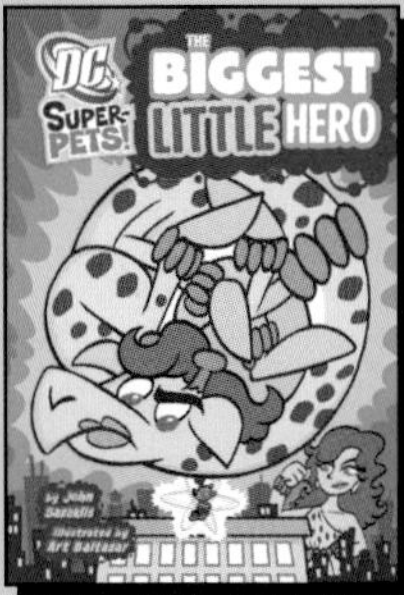
DC SUPER-PETS!
THE BIGGEST LITTLE HERO

SPOT!

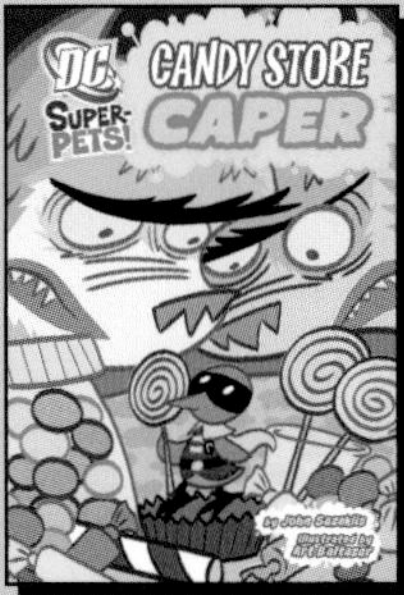
DC SUPER-PETS!
CANDY STORE CAPER

ROBIN ROBIN AND ACE TEAM-UP!

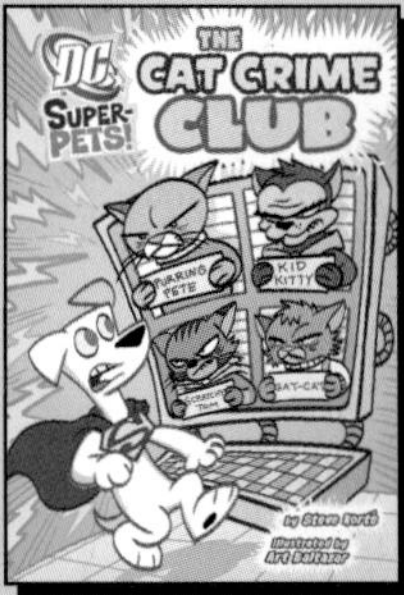
DC SUPER-PETS!
THE CAT CRIME CLUB

SPACE CANINE PATROL AGENCY!

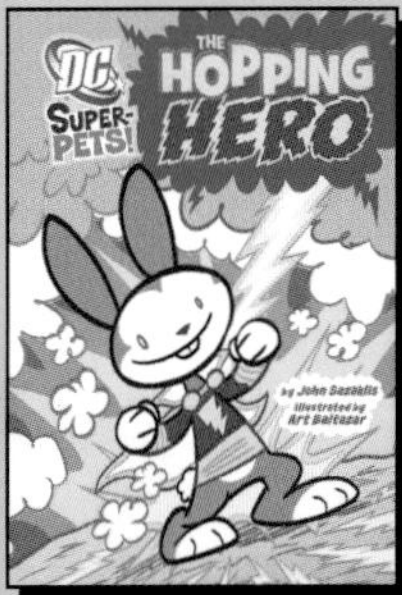
DC SUPER-PETS!
THE HOPPING HERO

HOPPY!

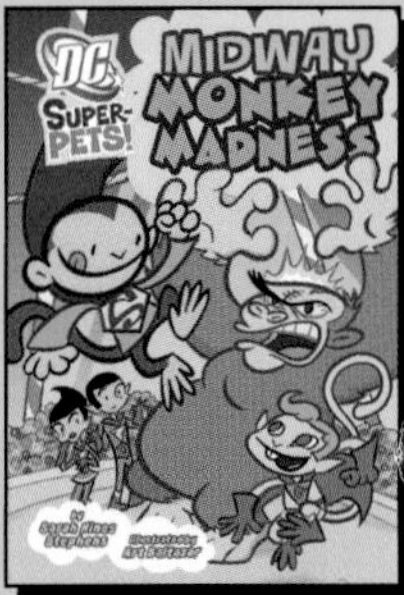
DC SUPER-PETS!
MIDWAY MONKEY MADNESS

BEPPO THE SUPER-MONKEY!

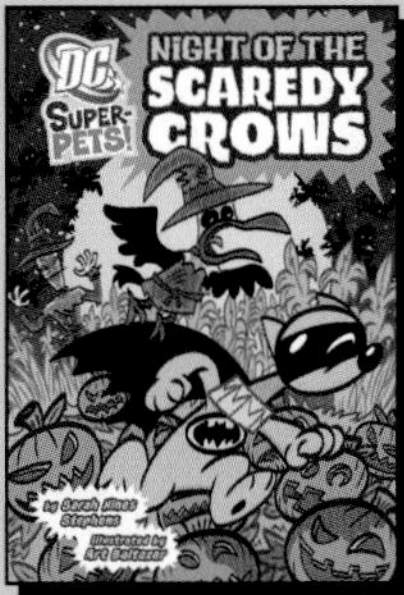
DC SUPER-PETS!
NIGHT OF THE SCAREDY CROWS

ACE THE BAT-HOUND!

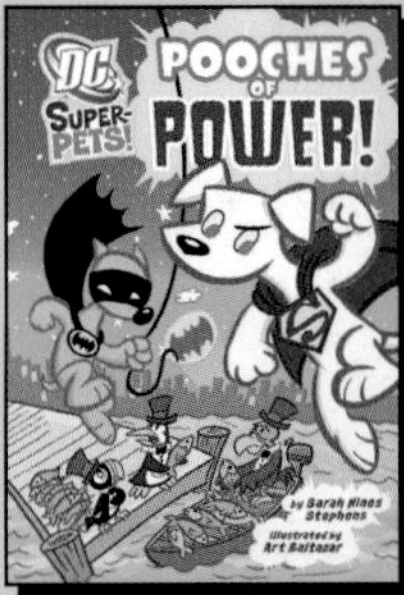
DC SUPER-PETS!
POOCHES OF POWER!

KRYPTO AND ACE TEAM-UP!

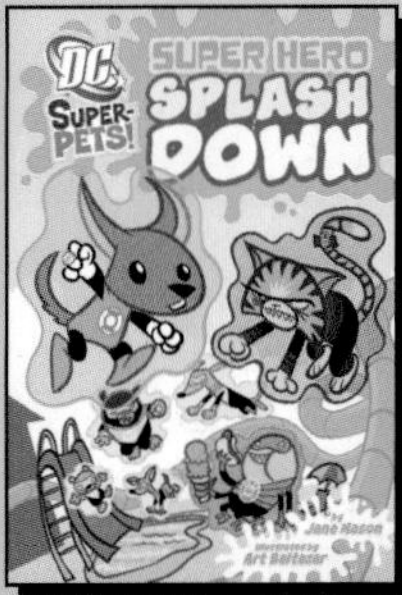
DC SUPER-PETS!
SUPER HERO SPLASH DOWN

B'DG, THE GREEN LANTERN!

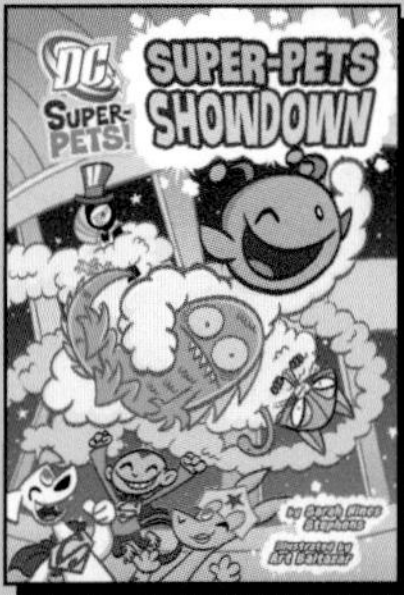
DC SUPER-PETS!
SUPER-PETS SHOWDOWN

THE LEGION OF SUPER-PETS!

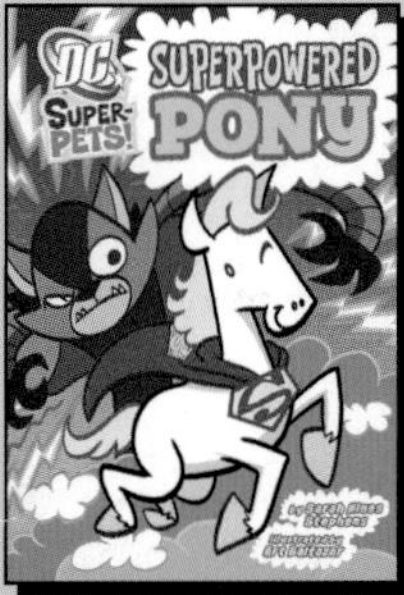
DC SUPER-PETS!
SUPERPOWERED PONY

COMET THE SUPER-HORSE!

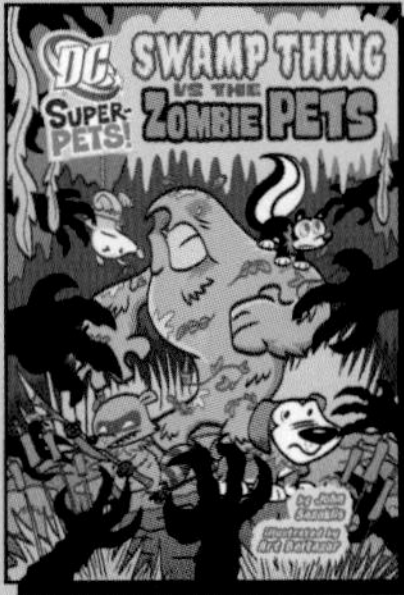
DC SUPER-PETS!
SWAMP THING VS THE ZOMBIE PETS

DOWN HOME CRITTER GANG!

Picture Window Books™

Published in 2012
A Capstone Imprint
1710 Roe Crest Drive
North Mankato, MN 56003
www.capstonepub.com

Copyright © 2012 DC Comics.
All related characters and elements are trademarks of and © DC Comics.
(s12)

STAR26102

Cataloging-in-Publication Data is available at the Library of Congress website.
ISBN: 978-1-4048-6492-4 (library binding)
ISBN: 978-1-4048-7663-7 (paperback)

Summary: It's Halloween in Gotham, but the streets are frightfully empty. The trick-or-treaters have all disappeared! Soon, Ace the Bat-Hound sniffs out a flock of feathered felons. These evil Scaredy Crows have coated the city in fear dust, scaring everyone away. Now, the Bat-Hound is Halloween's only hope!

Art Director & Designer: Bob Lentz
Editor: Donald Lemke
Creative Director: Heather Kindseth
Editorial Director: Michael Dahl

Printed in the United States of America in Stevens Point, Wisconsin.
032012   006678WZF12

DC™

SUPER-PETS!

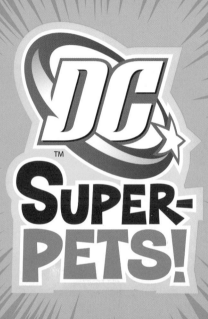

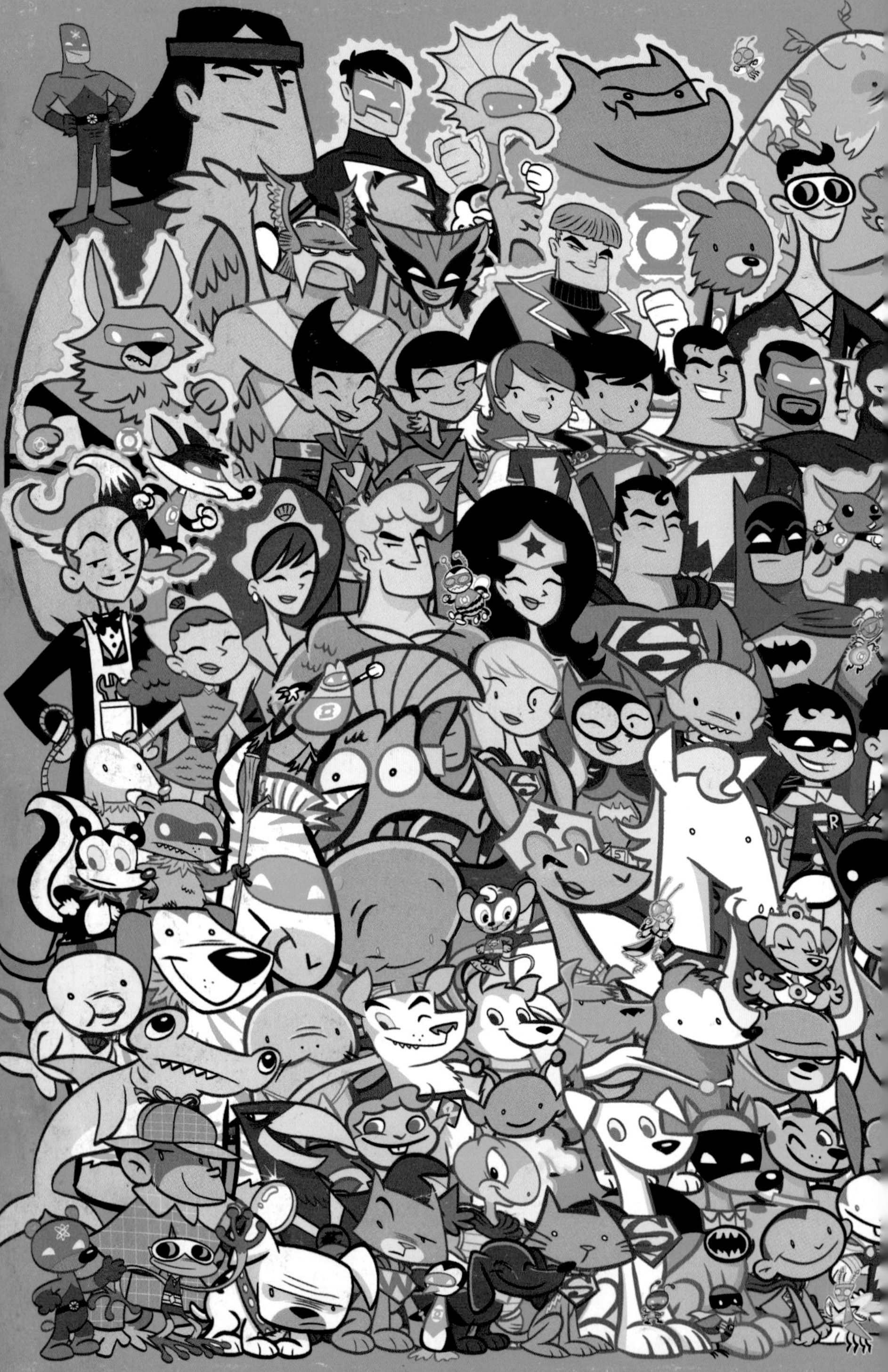